To my three favourite
little lions,
Amy, Ellie and Lizzie
E.C.

First published 2015 by Macmillan Children's Books.

This edition published 2018 by Macmillan Children's Books,

an imprint of Pan Macmillan

20 New Wharf Road, London N1 9RR.

Associated companies throughout the world.

www.panmacmillan.com

ISBN: 978-1-5290-0589-9

1 2 4 6 8 9 7 5 3

Printed in China

Lion Practice

Emma Carlisle

Macmillan
Children's
Books

My name is Laura and I love to practise.

I love kangaroo practice,

boing boing boing!

parrot practice,

flap flap flap!

and elephant practice too.

whooooosh!

And I'm VERY good at crocodile practice.
Everyone things so.

Mum says that today
I should practise being
something small and
quiet, like a mouse.

But I have a
much better idea.
Today I will try . . .

Lion
practice!

Lions walk on their hands and feet, like this . . .

And lions
have the
messiest
manes,
like this . . .

PERFECT!
But what else?

13

I think lions are
good at hiding,

and leaping,

and running VERY fast!

Oh, and I know,
lions roar REALLY
loudly, like this . . .

ROOAAAR!

But mum and dad didn't like my roaring, or my leaping. They told me to stop running around and keep the noise down.

"Oh dear . . .

I'm sorry . . .

I just . . .

. . . I just wanted to be a good lion."

Dad came out and found me . . .

. . . and then mum came too.

"Don't be sad, Laura," they said.

"Guess what we've been practising?"

BIG BEAR HUGS!

For our favourite
little lion."

A little lion?

A little LION!

What else do
little lions do?

Mum says they need a BIG dinner.

And dad says they need extra bubbles at bath time.

I say little lions
don't like pyjamas.

Mum and dad
say I can be a cheeky
monkey sometimes . . .

A cheeky monkey?
That sounds like fun!

I'm going to practise being
one of those tomorrow.